Jack
and the
Beanstalk

Illustrated by Dorothea King

Brimax Books · Newmarket · England

Jack and his mother were very poor.
One day, Jack went to market to sell
their cow. On the way, Jack met a man.
"Is your cow for sale?" asked the man.
"Yes, she is," said Jack.
"I will give you five magic beans
for her," said the man.
Jack took the beans and gave the cow
to the man. He hurried home
to his mother.

When Jack got home he showed
his mother the beans.
"You fool!" she cried. "What can we do
with those?" She snatched them from
his hand and threw them out
of the window. She would not listen
when Jack said they were magic beans.
"There are no such things as
magic beans," she said, and sent
Jack to bed without any supper.

How wrong she was. The magic beans
sprouted in the night and began
to grow. They grew so tall
that when Jack awoke the next day,
he found an enormous beanstalk
outside his bedroom window.
"I am going to see what is at the top,"
said Jack, and he began to climb.
"Be careful," called his mother.

Jack climbed higher and higher
up the beanstalk until at last
he reached the top. There he found
himself in another world, high above
the clouds. He walked along a path
until he came to an enormous house.
"I must be in a land of giants,"
said Jack as he knocked loudly
on the door. It was opened by
the wife of a giant.
"Come in," she said to Jack.
She gave him some breakfast.

Jack had just finished eating when
he heard heavy footsteps and a loud
voice shouting,
"Fee fi fo fum, I smell the blood
of an Englishman!"
"That is my husband," said the woman.
"He eats boys like you for breakfast.
Quick, hide in the oven."
Jack did as she said. He did not
want to be eaten by the giant.

The giant was sure he could smell
a boy, but he could not find him.
He had to eat porridge for breakfast
instead. When he had finished,
he called for his hen. Jack peeped
out of the oven.
"Lay, hen!" ordered the giant.
Jack watched and saw the hen
lay a beautiful golden egg.
'Mother would like to own a hen
like that,' thought Jack.

Jack waited until the giant was asleep,
then he crept from his hiding place.
He picked up the hen and tucked it
inside his shirt.
"You are coming home with me,"
he said. He ran from the house
without waking the giant
and climbed down the beanstalk.
"See what I have," he called
as his mother came to meet him.
"It lays golden eggs."

Next morning, Jack climbed up
the beanstalk again. When he reached
the giant's house he slipped under
the door.
"Fee fi fo fum!" roared the giant.
"I smell the blood of an Englishman!"
This time Jack hid in a drawer
and the giant had to make do with
porridge for his breakfast once more.
It made him very angry.

When the giant had eaten his breakfast,
he called for his harp. Jack watched
from his hiding place as the giant's
wife placed a small, golden harp
in front of her husband.
"Sing, harp!" the giant ordered.
The harp sang, but the giant
did not touch the strings once.
'Mother would like a harp like that,'
thought Jack.

At last the giant fell asleep, and Jack
crept out of the drawer. He reached
out his hand to pick up the harp,
but as soon as he touched it,
the harp called loudly,
"Master! Master! Wake up!"
At once the giant jumped up
from his chair. He roared with
anger when he saw Jack.
"Fee fi fo fum, I smell the blood
of an Englishman!"

Jack held on to the harp and dodged
between the giant's fingers and ran
as fast as he could to the top
of the beanstalk.
"Fee fi fo fum!" shouted the giant.
He was in a terrible rage.
As Jack climbed down the beanstalk,
he could feel it shaking and trembling
as the giant climbed down behind him.

Jack's mother heard all the noise
and came running from the house.
She was very frightened when
she saw the giant.
"Quick mother! Give me the axe!"
shouted Jack, as he jumped the last
few feet to the ground.
There was no time to lose.
He took the axe from his mother,
and with one mighty blow he cut
right through the beanstalk.

The beanstalk and the giant fell
to the ground with a great crash,
and made a hole so deep that they
were never seen again.
As for Jack and his mother,
they lived happily ever after.
And with the golden hen that could
lay golden eggs and the harp that
could sing by itself, they were
never poor again.